HOPELE~~S~~

ODYSSEUS'
TROJAN TRICK

STELLA TARAKSON

Sweet Cherry

Published by Sweet Cherry Publishing Limited
Unit 36, Vulcan House,
Vulcan Road,
Leicester, LE5 3EF
United Kingdom

First published in the UK in 2020
2020 edition

2 4 6 8 10 9 7 5 3

ISBN: 978-1-78226-352-4

© Stella Tarakson

Hopeless Heroes: Odysseus' Trojan Trick

Cover design by Nick Roberts and Amy Booth
Illustrations by Nick Roberts

www.sweetcherrypublishing.com

Printed and bound in Turkey
T.IO006

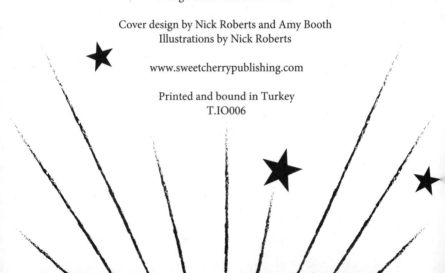

For Chris,

for being my big brother

Presented to

Noah

July 2022

For being a wonderful
member of Year 4

Reading sets
you free x

From Mrs King, Mrs
Boreham & Mrs Vyas

'Are you sure this is a good idea?' Tim Baker sat with his shoulders hunched. He stared glumly at his best friend Ajay, who was sitting opposite him. 'We've got no chance.' Tim grumbled.

'Don't be like that,' Ajay said. His brown eyes flicked up to Tim's face then back down again. 'We can do it. Now concentrate.' Ajay drummed his fingers on the tabletop and propped his chin on one fist.

Tim could tell that his friend was getting impatient, but he didn't like being pushed. 'Why did we agree to play in the first place?' he moaned. Beads of sweat had broken out on his brow and he wiped

them away with the back of his hand. 'We'll be like lambs to the slaughter.'

'Would you stop being such a misery guts?' Ajay said, inspecting the chessboard. 'We've as good a chance as anyone. Why are you so grumpy?'

'I'm not grumpy,' Tim muttered, even though he knew he was. There was no way he could tell Ajay the reason why.

He'd tried sharing his big secret with his friend back when his adventures first started, but Ajay hadn't believed him. Not many people would believe that the ancient hero, Hercules, had been trapped in an old Greek vase. Or that he'd escaped into the modern world when Tim accidentally broke it. Ajay had thought it was all a joke. So Tim never told him that he'd also worked out how to travel through time, back to Ancient Greece.

His best friend knew nothing about Tim's adventures with Zoe, Hercules' daughter. Ajay didn't know that Hera, the vengeful queen goddess, hated Tim and was always trying to capture him. This meant Tim couldn't tell Ajay the *real* reason for his grumpiness: he was worried.

Last night, Tim and Zoe had overheard her parents talking. They hadn't been able to catch everything, but they got the gist: Hera had threatened Agatha, Zoe's gentle mother, who had shown Tim nothing but kindness.

And it was all Tim's fault.

8

'Are you going to make your move or what?' Ajay's eyes flashed with annoyance. 'We haven't got all day, you know.'

Tim heard someone snigger. From the corner of his eye he noticed a figure lurking. He kept his gaze firmly on his chess pieces – he was not in the mood for an audience. Shrugging, he reached out his finger and pushed. 'Bishop to E5,' Tim said, his voice flat.

Ajay's eyebrows flew to the top of his forehead. 'Are you nuts? That leaves your queen wide open. See? I can get her with my rook.' He matched his words with the action.

Tim blinked at the checkered board. 'Oh yeah.'

If only Hera, Queen of Olympus, was that easy to defeat. Tim sighed. Hera feared and mistrusted the future. She wanted to rule forever in a world that never changed, where the Olympians reigned supreme. Yet Tim represented a time when they were all but forgotten. Hera seemed to hate him just for that. And it didn't help that he had defied her several times and won. Now, because Hercules was on Tim's side, Hera was threatening to do something to his wife. Tim didn't know what exactly – Zoe's parents wouldn't tell them – but that only made him worry more. How could he protect Agatha against an unknown threat?

'Are you listening?' Ajay asked tetchily. 'Look at the board. Checkmate in two moves.' He traced the paths his pieces could take with his fingers. 'Maybe you're right,' Ajay added, his lips falling into a frown. 'Maybe we should drop out of the chess club. We'll be a laughing stock.'

Ajay was the school's best player. Tim knew he had been looking forward to next week's match against the posh girls' school. Tim would have been too, if his life wasn't falling apart …

CRASH!

Tim jumped. The sound of the falling chess set was like a thunderclap in the quiet library.

'Hey! Watch it!' Ajay growled,
snapping around to face the large boy
who loomed over them.

'That's what you get for ignoring me,' Leo snapped, folding his arms across his chest. 'I don't like being ignored.'

Tim looked at Leo warily. Leo had been bullying Tim for years. Tim knew that Leo had problems at home, but that didn't make him any easier to deal with.

'Sorry, I didn't notice y–' Tim started to say, but Ajay interrupted him hotly.

'Can't you see we're busy?' Ajay said to Leo. 'We have to practice.'

'I don't know why you nerds waste your time on this stupid game. Hang on … yeah, I do. You're nerds.' Leo chuckled nastily.

'I'd like to see you do better,' Ajay snapped, scooping up the chess pieces that had fallen on the floor and piling them back onto the table.

'You're on,' Leo said. He pulled up a chair, turned it backwards and straddled it. 'I can beat you at your own stupid game. You first, Cinderella.'

'What?' Tim was surprised that Leo had taken the bait. So surprised that he barely noticed the nickname Leo always taunted him with – a jab at the fact that Tim had to do housework.

'SCARED?'

Leo sneered. 'Know you're going to lose, do ya? Chicken.' He flapped his arms as if they were wings and made loud clucking sounds.

'Shh, you'll get us kicked out of the library.' As he spoke, Ajay swiftly set up the board. 'You can play if you're quiet.'

Tim wondered whether Ajay wanted him to play against Leo so that he'd gain some confidence with an easy victory.

'Bagsy the white pieces.' Leo cracked his knuckles and picked up a white pawn. 'Tell ya what. If I lose, I'll stop calling you Cinderella.' His squinty eyes bored into Tim's. 'But if I win, you've got to do something for me.'

'What sort of something?' Tim asked suspiciously.

Leo shrugged his beefy shoulders. 'Dunno. I'll think of something.'

Tim peered at him through narrowed

eyes. He knew that Leo was on to him. Leo had been at Tim's house, working on a school project. Snooping around, he'd caught Tim on his way to and from one of his adventures in Ancient Greece. Tim had been avoiding Leo ever since, hoping he'd forget about it.

'Come on,' Ajay urged Tim. 'There's no way you can lose against him.'

But Tim did. Leo played cleverly and aggressively and won the match in just a few moves. Ajay, who'd been watching with his mouth hanging open, couldn't wait to challenge Leo himself. Minutes later, Ajay was left scratching his head in amazement as he, too, lost the game in record time.

'How come you're so good at this?' Ajay asked, his hair standing up in wild tufts. 'You should join the chess club! You can partner me in the match next week. We'll win for sure.' Ajay didn't ask whether Tim minded, he noticed.

'Might do,' Leo said carelessly, 'if there's nothing better to do.' Standing up, he cracked his knuckles. 'Don't forget you owe me a favour, Cinderella. See you after school – at your place.'

Tim grabbed his bag as soon as the bell rang. He wanted to get home as quickly as possible, before Leo could catch up with him. To thrash them so easily at chess, the bully couldn't be as dumb as he looked. He knew that Tim was hiding a mysterious secret, but he didn't know what it was.

Tim planned to keep it that way.

Ajay bustled up to him, a worried look on his face. 'You don't mind me asking Leo to partner me in chess, do you?'

'No. It's fine.' It came out more sharply than Tim intended.

'It's just that he's so good,' Ajay said, his eyes widening with worry. 'And you said you didn't want to play anyway …'

'I don't mind, really.' Tim flashed an oversized toothy grin, hoping to reassure his friend. Ajay flinched. 'No, really. It's a relief,' Tim added. 'I'm in a rush, that's all.' He swung his bag over his shoulder and checked that Leo hadn't followed him out of the classroom. He knew he'd be full of questions – questions that Tim did not plan on answering.

'Oh. Hey, what was all that about Leo coming to your place and–' Tim didn't hear the rest of Ajay's sentence. He was already running towards the school gate, without a backwards glance.

■ ■ ■

The magic vase was back on the mantelpiece in the living room. Mum had decided to sell it, and now that she'd found a buyer she'd decided that Tim couldn't keep it in his bedroom anymore. 'If you broke it once, you might break it again,' she had said, matter-of-factly. She still didn't know how Tim had managed to fix it so perfectly. The criss-crossing cracks that had once covered the glued-together surface had mysteriously

vanished, and now it looked as good as new. Of course he couldn't tell her that the messenger god Hermes had fixed it with a simple wave of his hand.

At least Mum hadn't locked the vase away. If she had, Tim would never know whether Agatha was safe.

Tim couldn't tear his eyes away from it. He knew he should be doing the dusting and then his homework. But how could he, when Zoe's mother was in danger? Hera might be after her at this very moment. Or maybe it was too late! Maybe the goddess had already done whatever it was she'd threatened to do.

Tim had to go back and help his friends. He wouldn't have the vase for much

longer. Now might be his only chance to fix the problem – once and for all.

Abandoning his chores, he grabbed the vase's black handles. 'Oh vase, take me to Zoe's place,' he said out loud. In his head he added, 'for one last time'.

His feet lifted into the air as the familiar golden mist shimmered around his body. The dizzying flight through time and space used to make him feel queasy, but now he found it unbearably slow. The vase deposited him on Zoe's doorstep and Hercules answered his knock.

'Tim Baker!' the hero boomed, his face crinkling into a delighted smile. 'I didn't think we would see you again. Welcome! Come inside.'

Tim stepped over the threshold into the internal courtyard. By the looks of it, everything was fine. He let out a shaky breath.

'Agatha and Zoe have gone to the well but they promised they wouldn't be long,' Hercules continued. 'Come with me into the andron. A friend of mine is here, and I think you know each other.'

Tim didn't move. He was still trying to calm his nerves. Besides, he'd never been in that room before. 'The andron? B-but … only men are allowed in there,' he stuttered. Women and children – even Agatha and Zoe – couldn't enter the mysterious room.

'That is true.' Hercules stared down at Tim, his face thoughtful. 'But you have changed a great deal since we first met. You have faced many monsters and outsmarted the gods themselves. My friend, I think you have earned your place inside.'

Tim pulled himself up to his full height. The andron! Wow! He'd always wondered what it was like. Zoe would be so jealous if she knew. Holding his breath, Tim followed Hercules inside.

The andron was easily the largest room in the house. A sprawling mosaic covered the floor, its white, grey and black pebbles set in geometric shapes. There were a dozen pictures painted directly onto the plastered walls, each showing Hercules performing one of his

twelve labours. Unlike the other rooms, which showed Agatha's gentle touch, this room was darker and distinctly masculine. Couches that looked like a cross between a bed and a sofa were arranged around the walls. On one of these, nestled among cushions, lounged a familiar figure.

'Tim Baker, youthful friend from the future, I salute you.' The powerful warrior propped himself on his elbow and raised his drinking cup. He was wearing gleaming bronze chest armour. His boar-tooth helmet was tucked beneath his seat. 'Will you be joining us in a toast? I assure you our host provides only the finest of wines.'

'No thanks, Odysseus,' Tim said, trying not to stare at his surroundings. 'I don't drink wine. I'm too young.'

The tanned, middle-aged warrior, who Tim had met on a recent adventure, raised a bristly eyebrow.

'TOO YOUNG?

You disappoint me. Did I say I was too young when I withstood the sirens' song? Did I say I was too young when I hurled a pointed stick into the Cyclops' single eye, thus blinding him and enabling our escape?'

Tim shuddered. That sounded awful. Suddenly he felt even younger. 'I'm only ten.'

'Fie! Did I say I was only ten when I cunningly devised the Trojan Horse and used it to defeat the enemy?'

'Wow, were you only ten then?' Tim asked.

'No ... but I fail to see how that matters. Did I say I was only ten when–'

'That will do, Odysseus,' Hercules interrupted, hands on hips. 'Leave the boy alone. Come, let us play a game of astragaloi to pass the time until the women return. Tim Baker may join us if he wishes.'

Not another game! Tim had been expecting grown-up talk, about battles or wars or something equally thrilling. He may as well still be in the library with Ajay.

Tim hoped that this new game was nothing like chess, and was relieved when Hercules pulled out a small cloth satchel. Inside were some knobbly little bones, which Tim recognised as knucklebones. His grandmother had a plastic set that she used to play with as a child. She would throw all the pieces in the air and catch them on the back of her hand. Tim had tried it a few times. It was harder than it looked. Hercules' set was different. There were numbers written on the bones, making them look a bit like dice.

'Do you know how to play?' Hercules asked, squatting on the floor.

'Dad, come quickly!'

Tim jumped when he heard Zoe's voice through the doorway. She sounded upset.

Hercules dropped the knucklebones and sprung to his feet. In one swift motion, he was out of the andron and in the courtyard. 'What's wrong?'

'It's Ma.' Tim caught a glimpse of Zoe's tear-stained face. 'She's gone.'

'What do you mean, gone?' Hercules
snapped. 'Where? How? Tell me what
happened.'

'We were on our way back from the
well,' Zoe started to say, 'and Hera–'

'Hera? I ordered her to stay away!'
Hercules slammed his fist into his
palm. 'I knew I should not have let your
mother go out today. I tried to warn her,
but she refused to listen. She said Hera

wouldn't dare touch her in full view of the townspeople.'

'Silence.' Odysseus flapped a hand at his friend. 'Continue, daughter of Hercules.'

Zoe gulped. 'Hera caught us in a side street. There was no one else there.'

'What happened?' Tim asked. He could feel his chest tightening.

'She told Ma that her time was up. We hadn't handed Tim over, so now we would pay the price.' Her eyes slid over to Tim and then quickly away.

Tim felt his blood run cold. His worries had been justified – his friends were in trouble because of him, and now it seemed the worst had happened.

'What did your mother say?' Hercules asked, his jaw tight.

'She told Hera to get lost! You should have seen her, Dad, she was magnificent. Ma stood up to her!' For a moment, Zoe's familiar defiance flashed across her face, before being replaced by sadness.

'What happened then?' Hercules gripped the door so tightly that the wood began to splinter.

'Hera got angry. She said we were being stubborn and foolish. She said we had no one to blame but ourselves. Then she snapped her fingers, and Ma dis–disappeared!' Zoe dissolved into tears.

'What did that old witch do with her?' Hercules demanded. 'Did she tell you?'

But Zoe was crying too hard to answer. Tim put his arm around her shoulder and squeezed. After a few moments she took a gasping breath, shook herself, and continued.

'She said she's keeping Ma prisoner in the fortress on the big hill. She told me to say that it's guarded by her special soldiers, and to say that– Oh Dad, she said we'd need an entire army to get her out.'

'Then we shall get an army!' Hercules roared, shaking his fist. 'The mightiest in all the land. We shall defeat the wicked goddess, and crush her so-called special soldiers underfoot as if they were ants. Odysseus, are you with me?'

The warrior placed a rough-skinned hand on the hero's shoulder. 'Until the end, my friend. Calm yourself and be of good cheer. Remember that I am Odysseus the wily, Odysseus the cunning, Odysseus the leader of heroes. We shall find a way to restore your good wife to you.'

'Well said! Let's go at once!' Hercules ripped the splintered door out of its frame and hurled it to the ground. He stepped onto the street, his face like a thundercloud.

'No, wait. We must consider our actions' Odysseus' voice remained steady. 'There is nothing to be gained from hurtling headlong to our own destruction. Let us return indoors and discuss the matter sensibly, as men of intellect.'

Zoe groaned and looked at her father, her eyes filled with tears.

Tim guessed that it was the 'men of intellect' remark that had her worried. Hercules might be super-strong, but he wasn't exactly super-smart. As for Odysseus – he called himself cunning, but was he *really*? All Tim had actually seen him do was brag.

Zoe wasn't allowed to enter the andron with the men. Hercules and Odysseus made her wait outside while they held their war council. Tim hesitated in the doorway, torn between wanting to join the men and wanting to comfort Zoe. He decided he would be of more use to his friend if he could help rescue her mother. Tim flashed Zoe a reassuring smile before entering the room.

'I am telling you, it has worked before.' Odysseus was sitting upright on his couch, his elbows propped on his thighs. 'It is the same cunning plan that won us the Trojan War!'

Hercules scratched his head. 'So tell me again. How would a giant wooden horse get us into the fortress?'

'It got us through the gates of Troy–'

'It only worked because the Trojans thought it was an offering to Athena!' Zoe's frustrated voice drifted into the andron. She couldn't enter, but clearly that hadn't stopped her from eavesdropping on the men's conversation.

'What?' Odysseus sounded tetchy at being interrupted.

'The Trojans thought Athena would be angry if they rejected the horse – that's why they took it in,' Zoe continued. 'But why would Queen Hera worry about the feelings of a lower-ranking goddess? She'd just leave the wooden horse outside.'

Tim looked at the heroes – they had to admit that Zoe had a point.

'The girl-child speaks true,' Odysseus said, leaning back on the couch. 'Hmm. There must be some other sort of large wooden structure that we could use to gain access. Can you suggest anything?'

Hercules closed his eyes and stroked his beard. 'A giant wooden Hydra?' He was referring to the many-headed sea serpent that Hera had once created to destroy him. 'No, she might magic it into life, and then we would have to fight it. We have to think of something that would be easy to defeat.'

Tim couldn't see why the goddess would want a giant wooden anything. All she cared about was power. Well, power and her birds.

'How about a wooden peacock?' Tim joked. The peacock was Hera's sacred symbol. Like other things sacred to the goddess, Hera had turned them into weapons. She had trained them to yowl whenever they saw Tim and Zoe, alerting her to their presence.

Hercules leapt to his feet. 'You are right, Tim Baker! Did I not tell you, Odysseus, that my friend is clever? We shall build a wooden peacock at once!'

'I was only joking,' Tim said. A wooden horse might have worked against the Trojans, but he didn't think the goddess would be so easily fooled – not even by a wooden peacock. 'Why would Hera want one? She's already got dozens of real peacocks.'

'We will call it a sacred offering,' Hercules said, ruffling Tim's curly hair. 'No god can resist an offering.' He rubbed his hands together. 'The battle is as good as won already.'

Odysseus nodded. 'We shall conceal ourselves in the peacock's belly, armed with our swords. Tim Baker will wheel us to the fortress' gate and announce the sacred gift. Then, after Hera's soldiers have admitted us through the walls, we shall spring from our hiding place. We shall slay the vile enemy and free your wife!'

Hercules pumped his fist in the air in agreement.

'But …' Tim still wasn't sure. 'Wouldn't it be easier to use ladders to climb the walls?'

Odysseus shook his head. 'Hera's guards would strike us down before we reached the top,' the warrior said gravely. 'Trust me, youth of the future, cunning trickery is our only hope.'

'But Hera's out to get me. We'll be walking straight into her trap!' As soon as the words left Tim's mouth, he felt ashamed. He didn't want them to think he was a coward. Besides, what choice did they have? They had to rescue Agatha.

Hercules seemed to guess what was on Tim's mind. 'Fear not, my friend,' the hero said, kneeling down so that he could look Tim in the eye. 'You shall wait outside the fortress while we men put the enemy to the sword.'

'Do not mollycoddle the boy.' Odysseus said, scowling. He picked up his boar-tooth helmet and crammed it over his head. 'Give him this opportunity to prove himself a man, and worthy of entering your  andron. Allow him to fight at our side and gain glory in battle.'

'Absolutely not. I will not hand him over to Hera,' Hercules said, drawing himself to his feet. 'Besides, he is only ten.'

 'FIE!'

Odysseus spat. 'Did I say I was only ten when I–'

'Don't start that again,' Hercules grumbled. 'We are wasting time.'

'You speak true,' Odysseus said, relenting. 'Let us build the wooden peacock without delay.'

'Yes. Let us.' Hercules paused. He looked around. 'Have you any wood?'

'No. I thought you did.'

'Me? What use have I for wood? I am a hero, not a carpenter.'

'Then what do you do in winter when you want to light a fire?'

'I pluck a tree out of the ground,' Hercules said, shrugging. 'I don't even use a saw to cut it up. I can get finer kindling by shredding it with my teeth.'

'Your teeth? How are we supposed to build a peacock with your teeth?'

'I'll have you know that my teeth are super-strong and super-sharp,' Hercules said, flashing a Hollywood smile. 'Nobody has mightier teeth than I!'

'I think you will find that I do.' Odysseus raised an eyebrow. 'Have you ever used your teeth to grip onto a rickety raft on a violent sea? My very life depended on the strength of my incisors–'

'How about we ask Jason?' Tim cut through the competition.

'Why?' Hercules asked, his arms folded across his chest. 'Do you think Jason's teeth are stronger than mine?'

Odysseus also looked offended at the mention of the boatbuilding hero.

'No,' said Tim slowly. 'I thought Jason might agree to build the peacock.'

'Oh, right,' said Hercules.

'Good idea,' muttered Odysseus.

■   ■   ■

Tim and Zoe had first met Jason when they were searching for the Golden Fleece. Tim was afraid that the young hero might be out sailing, but luckily he was at home tending to his beloved boat, the *Argonut*. It didn't take them long to convince him to take on a new project.

Zoe had refused to be left behind, and even Hercules couldn't stop her

from striding with the men to Jason's house. Now she stood silently with Tim, watching the wooden peacock being built. Tim caught Zoe's eye and she raised a sceptical eyebrow at him.

'I don't have any better ideas. Do you?' he whispered, so that only she could hear.

'Not yet.' She looked back at the peacock, and frowned.

Tim was impressed by Jason's skill as he sawed, sanded and hammered. To speed the task up, he was repurposing a hull from a previous project. He hummed happily as he worked, clearly relishing the new challenge.

Hercules, however, was not enjoying the process. He paced back and forwards anxiously. 'Can't you work any faster?' he barked. 'We haven't got all day!'

'Do you want quality, or do you want speed?' Jason asked, unfazed by the outburst.

'I want both!'

'Doesn't work that way, bro.'

'It works the way I say it—' Hercules started to say.

'How about you go wrestle a tree trunk or something, and let me get on with my work.'

'Wrestle a tree trunk?' Hercules boomed. 'Good idea. It will help me relax.' Flexing his muscles, the hero strode over to a mighty pine. He bounced on the balls of his feet, then flung himself hard and fast at the tree. 'Hah! This will teach you for standing there doing nothing while my wife is imprisoned!' he growled as he gripped the trunk in a bear hug. Pine needles showered to the ground as the tree creaked and flexed under the pressure. Zoe looked as if she didn't know whether to laugh or cry.

Eventually the frame of a gigantic wooden bird emerged before them, complete with a fanning tail and a dainty little head. All that was left was to line the body with planks of wood.

Hercules came bounding back, leaping over the trunks of several splintered trees. 'It doesn't look very realistic,' he grumbled, tilting his head left and right. 'Shouldn't it be life-sized?'

Jason bristled. 'Bro, you said you wanted to climb inside it.'

'Oh. Yes. Carry on.'

'What I wanna know,' Jason said, peering at the peacock's rear end, 'is will it float? That tail might throw it off balance. And where would I stick the sail?'

'It doesn't need to float,' Tim pointed out.

'Well, yeah. That's what you say now,' Jason ran a hand through his slicked back hair, 'but later you might change your mind. Later you'll say, "Bro, let's take this beauty for a ride!" And I'll have to say, "No can do, little bro, this beast won't float." And then you'll say–'

'Get. On. With. It.' Hercules was running out of patience.

'All right man, keep your cool. Sheesh!' Jason rolled his eyes and picked up another plank. 'But don't blame me if it sinks.'

'Remember to add a good trapdoor, lest we be trapped in the belly of the beast,' Odysseus said, patting the peacock's head. 'And sturdy wheels, so that we may transport it with ease.'

'I know, I know,' Jason grumbled. 'Hey, why don't you help out instead of just bossing me around? I'll show you what to do.'

'You expect me, the leader of heroes, to take instruction?' Odysseus' eyes bulged. 'Me, who rallied the troops after Agamemnon's dream? Me, who captained the ship that bore the fair Chryseis back to her father? Me, who—'

'If you want it done fast, then yeah.' Jason interrupted the warrior's rant with a uninterested wave of his hand.

'Leaders do not follow,' Odysseus said, nose in the air. 'I command you to make haste and complete your task without complaint. Unless you think you are not up to the challenge.'

'Not up to it?' Jason blinked. 'Of course I'm up to it. I'm just saying lend a hand to speed things up.'

'HE IS RIGHT.'

Hercules rubbed his hands together. 'Give me your tools at once, Jason. I shall super-help you.'

Tim recalled the time the hero had

super-swept Tim's home, and suspected Hercules would be more of a hindrance than a help. 'Maybe you can do the heavy lifting?' Tim suggested, not wanting to hurt his friend's feelings.

'Nothing could be easier.' Hercules began scooping up armloads of planks.

'That's more like it,' Jason said. 'And how about you, little bro? Care to lend a hand?'

'Just tell me what to do,' Tim said, stepping up to the peacock.

When it was completed, the wooden
peacock stood over ten feet tall. It
gleamed in the bright sunlight, its proud
head high. Jason had given Tim some
iridescent blue and green gemstones
to glue onto the tail, and he'd arranged
them to look like a peacock's eyespots.
Now, looking at their handiwork, Tim
was starting to think that their plan
might work after all. Hera might be

impressed enough by the offering to
accept it.

'How does the trapdoor work?'
Hercules asked. He rapped his knuckles on
the peacock's belly.

'OI, CAREFUL!'

Jason snapped at the hero. 'Use the lever
– see here? You pull it down. Gently.'
Jason matched the action to his words and
tugged on a hidden lever. The underside
of the peacock's belly lowered smoothly
to the ground, forming a ramp. 'After you
climb in, pull this rope to close the door.'

'Excellent,' Odysseus murmured,
peering into the hollow space. 'My
compliments to your skills as a craftsman.
This will easily fit all three of us.'

Jason puffed out his chest. Then, when
Odysseus' words sank in, 'Hey, what? All
three! Do you mean me or the kid?' He
jabbed his thumb in Tim's direction.

'The boy will wheel us there and present the gift to the guards. You have shown great skill in your work. In return we shall allow you to share our glory in battle.'

'No thanks, bro,' Jason said. He licked his index finger and held it up, testing the breeze. 'There's a sweet westerly wind blowing. I'm heading out to sea.'

'What did you say?' Odysseus took a threatening step towards Jason. 'You dare to go joyriding when there is an enemy to be slain? When a lady has been captured and awaits rescue?'

'Not my problem,' Jason replied serenely. 'I've done my bit. I'm off to ride the *Argonut*. Catch ya later.' He hoisted up his tools and turned to leave.

Hercules tapped the boatbuilder on the shoulder. 'First tell me one thing,' he said softly. Somehow he sounded far more menacing than if he had shouted. 'How do you expect to ride your boat, when it is smashed into tiny pieces?'

Jason twisted around. 'There's not *that* much wind. She'll be fine.'

'Not if I have anything to do with it.' Hercules cracked his knuckles.

Jason's usually tanned face turned a sickly white. 'That's not fair.'

'Fair? My wife is being held prisoner!' Hercules roared. 'Drop your tools, pick up your sword, and climb that ramp! At once!'

Tim was taken aback. Hercules often came across as goofy, but when the need arose he could be magnificent. Jason did as the hero ordered without further comment. Odysseus winked at Tim and clambered in after Jason.

Zoe cheered and pumped a fist into the air. 'Hooray! Save a spot for me,' she called after her father, who had stepped onto the ramp.

Hercules barely turned his head. 'Absolutely not. This is a job for men. Go home and prepare a victory feast for our return.' Zoe flushed an angry red as the hero climbed into the peacock and started to raise the ramp. 'Pick up the guide rope, Tim Baker, and take us to the fortress. For Agatha and for glory!'

Tim was surprised at how easy the wooden peacock was to manoeuvre once he got it going. Its wooden wheels rattled and the men inside shifted about, but the balance was perfect. Jason certainly knew what he was doing.

They came to the point in the road where Zoe was meant to turn off and go home. Instead, she pressed her lips together and walked grimly on, following close behind the wooden peacock. Tim looked at her but said nothing. Once she made up her mind about something, that was that.

Before long they reached the fortress at the top of the hill. Its high walls were made of large stone blocks. A stout

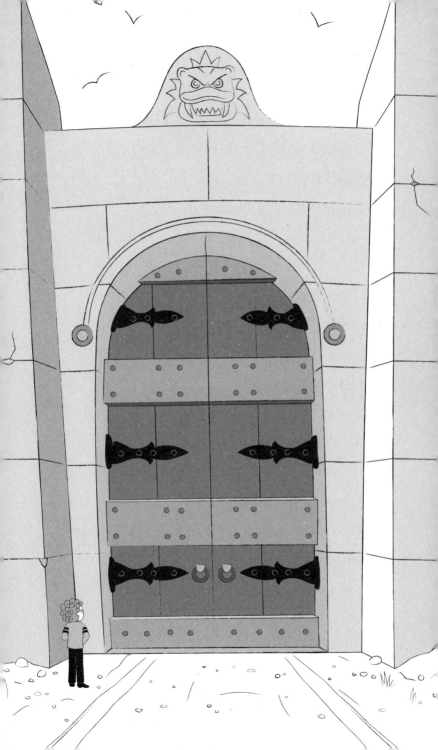

wooden gate barred the end of the path. Tim walked up to it, his heart pounding. He had expected it to be heavily guarded, but there was nobody there.

'What do I do?' he hissed from the corner of his mouth.

The peacock's belly creaked as the trapdoor eased open slightly. 'Knock, of course.' It was Odysseus' voice. 'Guards are likely to rush out at you, flourishing sharp swords and spears. Do not let that deter you. Once you have presented the gift, you may leave.'

'Err … okay.' Swords and spears? Tim gulped. What if the guards attacked him? He tapped gingerly at the gate and waited one heartbeat. 'There's no one home.'

'Do it like you mean it!' Odysseus ordered. 'Pound harder, with both of your fists.'

'All right …'

'Oh, let me.' Zoe tossed her ringlets over her shoulder and flew at the door. She pounded on it with her small fists, adding a few kicks for good measure. 'Open up! Come on, you guards, what are you waiting for?'

'Zoe!' The peacock shook alarmingly as Hercules' voice bellowed out of it. 'Is that you?'

'Yes it is. I'm here to save Ma,' she said, giving the door another kick.

'ITS OPENING!'

Tim shouted as the heavy gate started to swing open. He hoped the hero would hear him and realise that he had to be quiet, or else the plan would fail. The trapdoor snapped shut and no more sound came out of the wooden peacock.

The gate opened fully and Tim let out a squeak. Two guards stood before them, their spears crossed to form a barrier. They wore gleaming chest armour with panels shaped like sculpted muscles. They had knee-high shin guards and short pleated skirts. On their heads were bronze helmets with blood-red horsehair plumes, titled backwards to expose their scowling faces. From pictures he had seen on the Internet, Tim recognised them as hoplites:

heavily armed Greek soldiers. He gulped.
Hoplites were the best fighting force of
the ancient world.

'Who are you and what do you want?'
one of the hoplites demanded.

Tim fought hard to stop his knees from trembling. This was too important: his friends were depending on him to get them inside the fortress. He looked at the scowling hoplites, gulped and said, 'I-I've brought a tribute for Hera.'

The second hoplite looked at him scornfully. 'What, that pathetic heap of kindling? If it's not made of gold or silver, you're wasting our time.'

It was as he'd feared. Tim's shoulders drooped, but tensed back up when he heard an angry grunt from inside the peacock. It ended with a muffled squawk and wasn't repeated. Tim pictured an indignant Jason being silenced by either Hercules or Odysseus clamping a hand over his mouth.

'This magnificent offering comes from the finest craftsman in all of Greece,' Zoe jumped in. 'You're mad to reject it.'

'Hey, who are you calling mad?' the first hoplite said, thumping his spear on the ground. 'The cheek! Shouldn't you be at home with your mummy, little girl?'

Zoe tossed her ringlets over her shoulder. 'My mother? I'll have you know that at this very moment my mother is–'

'A devout follower of Queen Hera,' Tim interjected, before Zoe could lose her temper and give the game away. 'Her mother said Hera would be furious if she didn't get this offering.'

'Is that so?' The first hoplite looked wary.

Tim nodded vigorously. 'The goddess came to her mother in a vision and said: "Bring me a giant wooden tribute to my petals."' Tim used Hera's pet name for her peacocks. He hoped it would make the lie sound more plausible. 'And then she said, "Woe to the man who stands in its way."'

'Woe?' The guards exchanged anxious glances. 'Hmm. That sounds bad.'

Zoe pushed herself in front of Tim. 'Yes, woe! And then Hera said she'd make them pluck out their kidneys with their own dirty fingernails and eat them. Raw!'

Tim thought that was rather overdoing it, but Zoe's tactics worked. The hoplites flinched and the scowls dropped off their faces.

'I don't like kidneys,' the first one whimpered, his mouth puckering.

'Neither do I. Especially when they're my own. We'd better take it, just in case,' the second one said. 'What harm can it do? It's only a heap of wood.' The hoplites scrambled backwards, spears uncrossed. 'Enter, children, and leave your sacred offering for Queen Hera.'

'Ah, well, no.' Tim stumbled over his words. 'I'm, err, I'm not supposed to come in. I'm just meant to hand it over and then leave.'

The hoplites pointed their spears at Tim's throat. 'I said enter,' the guard said dangerously. 'The queen may wish to speak to you.'

'I'll take it in,' Zoe whispered to him, stepping forward. 'I'll be okay, Tim – Hera's after you, not me. You go home and wait for me there.'

'No chance. We'll go in together.' Squaring his shoulders, Tim picked up the peacock's rope and hauled it through the gate. Things weren't exactly going to plan, but at least he and Zoe had each other's backs.

'Hey, let me in!' Zoe snapped.

Tim whirled around. The hoplites had re-crossed their spears before Zoe could enter.

'The gift has been received,' the first hoplite said, turning his back on Zoe. 'Queen Hera might accept it or she might not. If she doesn't like it' – he looked meaningfully at Tim – 'you'll wish you were out there with the girl.'

With that, the gate slammed shut, silencing Zoe's protests.

'WAIT HERE,'

the second hoplite ordered, turning to go. 'We shall summon Her Majesty.'

Tim shuddered. Now what? All he could think of was finding somewhere to hide and wait until his friends emerged. He looked around. He was standing inside a barren, dusty courtyard. There was nothing to hide behind: no trees, no plants. A severe building loomed upwards, its heavy doors shut and its windows glaring like angry eyes. Could he hide in there?

'Timothy Baker,' said a silky voice. 'I knew it would be you.'

Tim looked up and saw Hera gliding towards him, her flock of birds following tamely behind. It was too late. He had to stick it out.

The goddess looked at the giant wooden peacock and pressed her thin lips together. 'Tell me, how do you come by this splendid offering?'

'I, err … Did you say splendid?' Tim was taken aback. 'You mean – you like it?'

'Indeed I do,' Hewra purred. 'Who is it from?'

'Hercules sent it,' Tim said, thinking rapidly. His heart pounded in his chest. Everything depended on him now. An idea flashed into his head and he blinked. 'He's – he's offering you a gift in exchange for his wife,' Tim spluttered. 'Take the peacock and let her go.'

If this new plan worked, Agatha would be freed and the heroes would hopefully escape unnoticed. There'd be no need for a fight.

'Mmm.' Hera stroked the smooth wood. 'It is most appropriate. A gift fit for a queen.'

'Does that mean you'll agree to a swap?' Tim asked eagerly.

'Perhaps,' Hera said, running her fingers over the iridescent gemstones. 'I must say I am tempted. However, there is one problem with wood. Do you know what it is?' She fixed Tim with a cold gaze.

'Um … splinters?'

'No,' She sighed regretfully. 'The problem with wood is that it burns so easily.'

And with a click of Hera's fingers, the wooden peacock burst into flames.

7

Tim jumped back in horror as the peacock burned. 'Get out of there!' he yelled.

The trapdoor sprang open and the heroes climbed hastily out of the peacock's belly. Their chitons were badly singed, and a wisp of smoke curled out of Hercules' beard.

'Argh! My beautiful bird!' Jason clutched his head as the fire crackled and popped. 'Now I'll never find out if she floats.'

'How dare you insult my intelligence,' Hera hissed at them, her face as stiff as marble. 'As if I would be stupid enough to fall for the old wooden animal trick!'

'It worked perfectly well during the Trojan War,' Odysseus said huffily. He readjusted his boar tooth helmet, which had slipped sideways in his rush to exit the inferno.

'Indeed, it was the key to our glorious vict–'

'Silence!' Hera clapped her hands together.

The sound was like a crack of thunder and Odysseus winced. He pressed his lips tightly together, restraining himself from answering back.

'You fools, you have walked straight into my trap.' Hera spun around to face Hercules. 'I warned you that I would take your wife, did I not? That I would have my revenge for the way you helped Timothy Baker evade me. I meant what I said!'

'Where is my wife?' Hercules roared, his entire body trembling with rage. 'If you have harmed so much as a single hair on her head, I shall wreak such vengeance –'

'Your wife is safe.' Hera curled her lip. 'If you had half a brain, you would know that I cannot harm her. After all, I am the goddess of women and marriage.'

The goddess clicked her fingers and a door in the towering building flew open. Agatha emerged. Her clothes and hair were as sleek and elegant as ever, and she didn't appear to have been hurt in any way. Seeing her husband, she rushed across the courtyard and into his arms. Hercules buried his nose in her hair and hugged her tightly.

'How romantic,' Hera sneered. 'What a shame this reunion will be short-lived.'

'What do you mean?' Agatha asked.

'I have what I want,' the goddess replied. 'Timothy Baker is trapped in my fortress forever. As a bonus, I have the oaf Hercules and some dim-witted mortals.'

'Who are you calling dim-witted?' Odysseus said, gripping the sword that hung from his belt. 'I am known for my wily intelligence. People call me Odysseus the Cunning, Odysseus the Leader of Heroes!'

'DO. NOT. SPEAK.'

Hera pointed a bony finger at the warrior. 'And if you dare to threaten me with that sword, I shall strike you down at once.'

Odysseus lowered his hand and fell silent. 'That's better.' The goddess turned back to Agatha and her voice softened. 'Your daughter waits outside the gate. Take her home, where you both belong. In the fullness of time, I shall send you another husband. Someone to replace the insolent oaf you so unwisely selected.'

'Never.' Agatha clutched Hercules more tightly. 'I will never forsake my husband.'

Hera's pale blue eyes were like chips of ice. 'I will not make this offer again. Go now, before I decide to keep you here forever. Your daughter will be alone in the world. Is that what you want?'

'Agatha, go,' Hercules said, stroking his wife's hair. 'Don't worry about me. I'll be out of here in no time.'

'Hah! Empty words,' Hera spat. 'It matters not. Leave at once, woman, and take your daughter home while you have the chance.'

With an agonised sob, Agatha tore herself out of her husband's arms. She ran towards the gate, where the hoplites were standing guard. They opened the wooden door and with one last glance at Hercules and Tim, Agatha left the fortress.

Hercules let out a mournful sigh as he stepped closer and placed a protective hand on Tim's shoulder. 'What are you planning to do with us?' Hercules asked.

❧❧

'With you?' The goddess shrugged. 'You can sit here and rot as far as I'm concerned. As for Timothy Baker, well ... I think a visit from an old friend of mine is in order.'

'What friend?' Hercules demanded. 'You don't have any friends.'

Hera raised an arched eyebrow. 'There is still one gorgon left, is there not?'

Tim felt his blood run cold as he remembered the gorgon he'd helped defeat. One glance from Stheno's eyes could turn you to stone. Her sister Medusa had been killed by Perseus many years ago. But Tim was pretty sure that Hera was right – there was still one gorgon sister left.

'You know, I would like a nice statue in my fortress garden,' Hera said comfortably. 'Brighten things up a bit. It will be a monument to my victory. Let me see, what shall I call it? The Boy from the Future?' The goddess cocked her head as if considering. 'No. I know. I shall call it The Boy with No Future.'

Hercules' grip on Tim's shoulder tightened.

'I shall go summon Euryale, the gorgon,' Hera continued, fixing Tim with her icy stare. 'Until then, contemplate what it will feel like to have your flesh turn to stone, to stand cold and lifeless for all eternity.'

A whimper escaped Tim's lips.

'And do not even think about escaping,' Hera said. 'I have an entire army of hoplites at my disposal.'

'Fie!' Odysseus sneered. 'We are more than a match for any army. We are heroes!'

Hera aimed an unpleasant smile at them, but her next words seemed to be directed at the sky.

'OH, HERMES ...'

she called.

At first nothing happened. The queen goddess looked almost comical as she began to tap her foot impatiently. Finally, the messenger god swooped in beside her.

'Yes, Your Majesty?'

'I want you to keep watch above my castle,' Hera instructed him. 'If the prisoners attack my hoplites, you are to fetch my son. He'll know what to do.'

The three heroes exchanged worried looks. 'Yes, Your Majesty. Right away, Your Majesty.' But then Hermes paused.

'Well? What are you waiting for?' the goddess thundered. 'Get up there!'

'Yes, but which–'

'NOW!'

Grumbling, Hermes launched himself into the air.

'What makes you think your son can stop us?' Odysseus demanded.

'If you sit there nicely like good boys, you need never find out.' Hera's voice dripped honey. 'But if you misbehave … well, let's just say he has a fiery temper.'

Smiling maliciously, she levelled a bony finger at Odysseus. 'Your legacy will be in flames.' The finger spun to Jason, 'your boatyard will be in ashes.' The finger dropped along with her tone, 'and Hercules' beloved wife and daughter will be dead.'

With a triumphant smile, the goddess clicked her fingers and disappeared, leaving Tim and his friends under the keen gaze of the gate guards, and Hermes circling overhead.

Tim stood frozen, as if he'd already been turned to stone. 'Hera's bluffing, right?' he asked. 'She can't hurt Agatha and Zoe. She said so herself.'

'That doesn't mean she can't get someone else to,' Hercules said. 'I believe she was talking about her son Hephaestus, the god of fire. She can make him set off volcanos if she so desires. When it comes to vengeance, Hera knows no bounds.'

Head hanging down, the hero trailed into a corner of the courtyard and slid to the ground. 'No. We cannot risk having the whole town destroyed by lava. We are stuck here. I have failed you, my friend. I have failed everybody.'

Tim followed his friend. 'No, you haven't. We'll think of something. We'll get out of here.'

The hero didn't respond. Instead he stared sightlessly at the ground, smudges of soot covering his cheeks. Tim had

never seen him look so dejected.

'I think it best if you leave him alone,' Odysseus said, guiding Tim away. 'Hercules fears he'll never see his family again. This is not the first time it has happened. He was trapped in the vase for thousands of years, remember? He believed he'd never see Agatha again. I know how he feels. I was away from my beloved wife Penelope for twenty years. Although I experienced great adventures, my heart ached every single day. There is nothing you can say or do that will ease his pain.'

'I understand. But, I can't just sit here waiting to be turned to stone! I mean, I know the Golden Fleece can cure me, but

I left my glove at home!' Zoe had the other glove, but how would she even know that Tim needed it? Let alone find a way to get it to him.

Odysseus laid a reassuring hand on Tim's shoulder. 'Do not worry. We will not let the gorgon hurt you.'

'There's got to be something we can do,' Tim said stubbornly. 'We can't just wait here like sitting ducks.'

'If the gods have it in for you, you're stuffed.' Jason spoke with an air of finality. He still clutched a smouldering chunk of timber from the wooden peacock's tail, the only part to survive the fire.

'Perhaps, in time, a solution will become clear to us.' Odysseus said.

'Hermes may grow weary of watching over us, or he may fall behind in his messenger duties. He might leave us temporarily unsupervised. Then we shall seize our chance. Until then, you must learn patience. I was once kept prisoner by the nymph Calypso for seven years before I found a way to escape.' The warrior eased his back against the fortress wall as if settling in for a long wait. 'We've been here for less than an hour.'

Seven years! Tim couldn't imagine being imprisoned for that long. By the time they escaped he'd almost be an adult! He knew the magic vase would take him home to a time just moments after he'd left – but how would Mum react if he strolled through the door suddenly aged 17? His voice would be deep and he might have a beard. She wouldn't believe it was him. She might even call the police!

'If only we had a game to pass the time,' Odysseus said, twiddling his thumbs. 'If I'd known we'd be detained thus, I would have brought my astragaloi set.'

Tim recalled the game of knucklebones that Hercules and Odysseus were playing with in the andron. It felt so long ago.

'Bro, how about these?' Jason pulled a cloth bag out of the folds of his chiton. He loosened the string to open the pouch and carefully poured out some of the contents. Large, sharp teeth gleamed in his hand. 'These belonged to the Colchian

Dragon – the beast that guarded the Golden Fleece. I kept them as a souvenir after I slew it. Lucky charms for good sailing, know what I'm saying?'

Odysseus grunted and shuffled closer. 'They will do, I suppose. Thank you, Jason, I will take five.' The warrior took the dragon teeth and placed them on the back of his hand. With a frown of concentration, he flipped his hand over so quickly that he caught all five in his palm. 'Hah! Excellent. I have lost none of my dexterity. Tim Baker, you have a turn.'

'This is silly.' Tim said. 'We're wasting time.'

'Patience, remember?' Odysseus handed over five teeth.

Tim balanced them reluctantly on the back of his hand, which was still trembling more than he cared to admit. He threw the teeth in the air and–

'Oops!' Tim only managed to catch one. The rest scattered across the dusty ground.

'Smaller movements, like this.' Odysseus demonstrated with his set, again catching all five with ease. 'Do not throw the teeth so high.'

Nodding grimly, Tim gathered the teeth and tried again. This time, he didn't catch any.

'Try flicking your wrist,' Jason advised, scooping up the teeth. 'Ready?

Go again.'

Tim managed to catch another one.
The other four rolled away. One wedged
itself in a crack in the ground and
wouldn't come out.

'Don't worry about it, little bro,' Jason
said. 'We've got hundreds. That dragon

had a big mouth.' He dug a few more teeth out of his bag. 'Take these.'

Grimacing, Tim tried again. He was so focused on the game that he barely noticed the armed soldier spring up out of the ground.

Startled, Tim felt his heart leap in his chest. The soldier was dressed like Hera's gate guards. It was another hoplite! Instead of a red helmet plume, this one had a snowy white one. Odysseus lurched backwards in surprise, and Jason dropped his bag of dragon teeth.

'Whoa, where did you spring from?' Jason asked, looking around warily.

The hoplite said nothing but pointed to a spot on the ground. He didn't seem aggressive. He surveyed them gravely through the eyeholes in his helmet. When he saw the battle-scarred Odysseus, the soldier walked smartly up to him, stood to attention, and flicked a salute. 'Awaiting your orders, sir,' the soldier said.

Quickly regaining his composure, Odysseus pulled himself to his feet. He stroked his chin as he circled the hoplite, examining him from head to foot.

'Humph. Not bad for one so young,' the warrior admitted. 'You look a little like my old friend, Achilles. Have you heard of him? He was a fearsome fighter but rather down at heel.'

'Yes sir, thank you sir,' the hoplite said.

'Why are you here? Who sent you?' Odysseus asked.

'Sorry sir, I do not know. I was just created, sir.'

Just created? What on earth did that mean?

Odysseus drew closer to Jason and the men talked in low voices. They scratched their heads and rubbed their chins. They looked from the white-plumed hoplite to Hera's gate guards, trying to gauge their reaction. The guards hadn't moved from their post, but Tim had the impression that they, too, were surprised by the hoplite's sudden appearance. They lowered their helmets into place in readiness to fight and picked up their shields, which had a giant letter 'H' written on them. H for Hera, Tim guessed.

Hercules continued to sit, unspeaking and unseeing.

Tim walked over to the patch of ground that the soldier had pointed out. It was the exact spot where the dragon tooth had wedged. Was that a coincidence? Experimenting, Tim picked up another tooth. He dug a hole in the dirt with the heel of his shoe and dropped the tooth inside. He watched intently and before long ...

POP!

Another white-plumed hoplite appeared. He went and stood beside the first.

'Awaiting your orders, sir,' the second hoplite said, saluting Odysseus.

The warrior and the boatbuilder looked taken aback.

'It's the dragon teeth!' Tim called out. 'When you plant them, they turn into soldiers!'

Jason reacted first. 'Little bro, that's brilliant! Quick, let's plant more.'

'But Hera said if we fight—'

'This is defence, Tim Baker, not offence,' Odysseus said. 'We will not fight. Instead, we can use the hoplites to guard you and protect you from the gorgon.'

Tim wasn't convinced by Odysseus' argument, but he needed to do something. He helped the two men sow the dragon teeth as quickly as they could. Each tooth took ten seconds to sprout. Soon soldiers were erupting all around the courtyard, like popcorn kernels popping in a pan. Odysseus rubbed his hands together as the soldiers obediently formed a group in front of Tim: side-by-side, shields interlocked, spears at the ready. Tim felt as though he were standing behind a fence of spears. As long as the tooth soldiers kept their eyes shut, they might just be able to hold off the gorgon.

The noise and activity finally broke through Hercules' melancholy. He looked up, shocked, then sprang to his feet. 'What are you doing?' he boomed. 'What about Hephaestus?'

'As I was saying, this is a matter of defence,' Odysseus started, 'not–'

'Tell that to Hermes!' Scowling, Hercules pointed at the sky.

Tim gulped. There was no sign of the messenger god. He must have left already!

'He's gone to get Hephaestus! What are w–'

Tim's voice faltered as he looked back at his friends. He hardly recognised them. Odysseus' face had stiffened, his eyes narrowing as he drew his sword. Jason, too, looked different. Older. Harder. As Tim watched, Hercules strode towards his friends and stood by their side, fists clenched, teeth gritted. What was happening to them?

A great shout came from the other end of the courtyard. Hundreds of red-plumed hoplites appeared and flooded the courtyard. Locked together in a solid group, they charged. The black Hs on their shields stood out starkly. Hera's army!

'GAH!'

Tim yelled, stepping back in shock.

Odysseus shouted a command that Tim couldn't hear over the howling war cries. The white-plumed soldiers must have heard though, because they charged back at Hera's hoplites. Shields clanged and spears flew as the two sides met. Hercules and Jason gleefully joined the fray.

Tim pressed himself against the fortress wall and watched in fascinated horror as the soldiers battled. Shields pushed against shields, but the formations held. It was like watching two brick walls trying to knock each other over. At first their side seemed to be winning, then Hera's side gained ground.

Tim kept having to move away as the battle heaved from side to side. There wasn't much space separating him from the fighting soldiers – if he reached out, he could almost touch their sweaty arms. It was only a matter of time before Tim ran out of room and the battle was on top of him. He tried scuttling into a corner where the fortress walls met but that was worse. He felt trapped. Sucking in his stomach, Tim edged his way along the other wall adjoining the gate.

It was then that movement on top of the wall to his right caught Tim's eye. It wasn't the goddess or gorgon coming to get him. It was a man. Tall and athletic looking, he leaned forward, watching

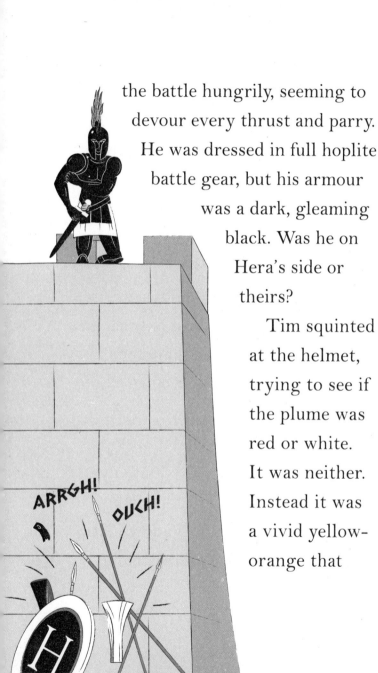

the battle hungrily, seeming to devour every thrust and parry. He was dressed in full hoplite battle gear, but his armour was a dark, gleaming black. Was he on Hera's side or theirs?

Tim squinted at the helmet, trying to see if the plume was red or white. It was neither. Instead it was a vivid yellow-orange that

ARRGH!

OUCH!

moved and flickered in a peculiar way. The plume was made of fire! Rather than coloured horse-hair, fierce flames shot from the top of the man's helmet. It had to be Hephaestus! As if feeling Tim's shocked gaze, the man turned to him, nodded, and disappeared.

Tim's pulse beat hotly in his ears.

A spear landed near his feet, making him jump, and a strange surge of excitement flooded through him. His hand seemed to move of its own accord – towards the spear. Part of Tim knew that it was crazy. What could a skinny ten-year-old boy do against well-trained, armoured soldiers? The other part told him that didn't matter. He wanted to fight!

Nobody was paying him the slightest bit of attention. That gave him an advantage. If he could pick up the spear ... circle to the side ... thrust unexpectedly ...

Tim's heart thudded as he reached for the weapon, fingers grasping it eagerly. He pulled. It didn't budge. He pulled again. Nothing. The spear felt like it was rooted to the ground.

The strange, electrifying feeling left Tim's body as quickly as it had come. He leapt back, eyeing his own hand like it belonged to someone else. What was he thinking? He couldn't fight! He'd have to find another way to help his friends.

He looked at the gate. The guards had joined the battle, leaving it unattended. Tim wondered whether it was locked from the inside. Unseen, he sidled along the wall, then dashed to the gate. It had a heavy latch. He pressed hard against it and it shifted upwards. They could escape! He had to tell Hercules.

It wasn't hard to work out which of the fighters was his friend. Hercules was so tall that he towered over the others.

Gathering his courage, Tim ran up behind him and tugged at his tunic.

The hero spun and thrust his sword at Tim.

'ARGH!'

Tim shouted as he leapt backwards.

'Tim Baker! Never do that again! I might have hurt you.' Hercules sounded shaken. He picked Tim up and plonked him back against the wall, where the fighting was less intense. 'Stay here and wait for me to finish them off.'

'The gate!' Tim pointed. 'We can leave!'

Hercules shook his head. 'Not yet. I'll quickly defeat this army, and then we can go.'

'B-but what about Hephaestus?'

'Hera lied – there is no sign of him.'

'But Hermes left, remember?' Tim pointed at the sky. 'He was following Hera's orders, and I'm pretty sure I just saw her son! What about Agatha and Zoe? The volcano might go off at any moment! And I don't want to be here when the gorgon turns up either. Nor should you. What if we're all turned to stone?'

Tim could tell that the hero was torn. Hercules glanced at the gate and then back at the hoplites. 'It is dishonourable to leave a fight before it is over,' he said.

'What's more important?' Tim shouted over the raging battle. 'Your honour or your family and friends?'

Conflicting emotions flickered across Hercules' face. 'My family and friends,' he finally admitted, bowing his head as if ashamed.

'Thank the gods.' Tim was relieved. 'Let's go.'

'It isn't right. I … I shouldn't.'

'You have to. We'll leave the others to carry on.' Tim grabbed Hercules' hand. The hero didn't shake him off. Face downcast, he groaned and turned towards the exit.

Guessing their move, a group of Hera's hoplites had broken away from the formation. They stood, shields up, forming a barrier across the gate.

'We shall have to fight our way out,'
Hercules said through gritted teeth.
'And when I say "we", I mean "I". Stand
back, Tim Baker. I don't want you to get
hurt.'

Tim stared at the row of Hera's
hoplites that stood barring the gate.
Silent, watchful, ready for action. 'You
can't fight them all,' he said. 'There are
too many of them!'

'Hah! That has never stopped me before!' Hercules cracked his knuckles. 'I had no trouble driving off a flock of man-eating birds. There were far more of them.'

Tim couldn't help thinking that a bunch of angry birds wasn't the same as an army. The hoplite's overlapping shields protected them and their neighbours. Any attempt to attack them would not only be futile, it would be met by a swift barrage of spears. Tim gulped. If the hoplites stayed together, they would be impossible to defeat.

If the hoplites stayed together …

If …

Tim had an idea.

'Wait here a sec,' he called.

As fast as he could, Tim scrambled back to where they'd been playing knucklebones a short time ago. He scanned the ground, looking for Jason's cloth bag. Maybe there were some dragon teeth left. Surely they hadn't buried all of them! All Tim could see was dirt, gravel and scuff marks where the hoplites had charged back and forth over the patch of ground. Tim looked around in desperation. Finally, he spotted the cloth bag. It had been kicked over to the fortress wall, where it lay tattered and covered in dust. He ran towards it.

'Please let there be some left,' he whispered, fingernails digging into his palm.

Tim grabbed the bag and his stomach sank. The bag felt light, flat and empty.

He had to make sure, though. Turning the bag inside out, he shook it vigorously. A handful of dragon teeth had been caught in the seams and fell onto the ground. Tim shouted in triumph and scooped them up.

'I'm coming,' he called out to Hercules. 'Don't do anything yet!'

Tim ran to the hero's side. They stood facing the hoplites, who raised their spears, preparing to strike. Tim closed his hand round the teeth, careful not to grip too hard. They were pointy and sharp and could easily draw blood. He lifted his hand and wished he were better at bowling.

Tim tried to remember what the school's cricket coach had taught him about throwing. Twist your upper body, use your hips to push yourself forward. He did it, but wobbled a little bit.

'Tim Baker, are you all right?' Hercules sounded alarmed.

'Shh!' Tim focused on the hoplite's widely spaced feet. Raise your bowling arm – no! Your non-bowling arm. Swing it down fast, at the same time whipping your bowling arm over and forward. With a snap of the wrist and a cry of exhilaration, Tim sent the teeth flying straight at the enemy. They scattered into the scuffed up dirt. The hoplites stamped their heels as they uttered a battle cry, pushing the dragon teeth deeper into the ground.

'They're going to charge. Get behind me,' Hercules said, lifting his arm to shield Tim.

Tim didn't reply and he didn't move. He was counting.

ONE. TWO. THREE. FOUR.

The guards pointed their spears at Tim and Hercules and their cries grew louder.

FIVE. SIX. SEVEN.

It was worse than waiting for the kettle to boil.

EIGHT. NINE.
TEN.
POP! POP! POP
POP POP!!!

White-plumed hoplites erupted
between the feet of Hera's soldiers,
knocking them over in the process.
Destabilised, the group fell apart as the
soldiers struggled to get up, their heavy
shields and armour hampering them. Even

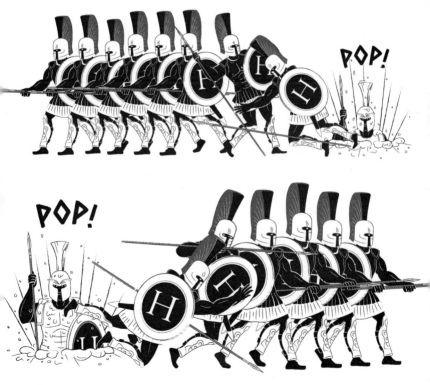

so, Tim knew it was only a matter of time before they regrouped and went on the attack.

'RUN!'

he shouted at the hero. 'Through the gate!'

Hercules didn't need to be told twice. He picked Tim up and threw him over his shoulder, as if he were a sack of feathers. Tim felt the air whoosh out of his lungs. He clung on tightly as Hercules charged at the gates, pushing over any hoplites who stood in the way. Tim heard a muttered curse as the hero hurriedly pulled up the gate's latch, then a creak of hinges, and the slam of a heavy door.

They were out. They had escaped from the fortress!

'We did it, Tim Baker!' Hercules said, lowering Tim gently to the ground. 'But we must go quickly. Once Hera realises you are missing, she will send her soldiers

after us. We will find Agatha and Zoe. Then you will stay out of Hera's way with them, and I will rejoin my friends to end the battle.'

The hero broke into a jog, and Tim had to run as fast as he could to keep up. Hercules kept his gaze firmly on the ground, while Tim checked left and right, on the lookout for Hera. They were almost home when Tim noticed the statues.

At first Tim didn't give them much thought. Just another pair of life-sized statues. That sort of thing was everywhere in Ancient Greece, right?

Well ... maybe not.

Slowing down, Tim turned back for a closer look. A shiver ran down his spine.

Despite the looks of horror plastered on their faces, he had no trouble recognising Zoe and Agatha.

11

Hera had lied! Tim gaped at the statues. She hadn't allowed Zoe and Agatha safe passage after all. She must have used the gorgon to turn his friends to stone before returning to do the same to him. Tim waved a hand under Zoe's nose, hoping for some reaction. There was none. The girl's eyes stared blankly ahead.

Hercules must have noticed that Tim was lagging behind. 'Hurry along, Tim

Baker,' he said over his shoulder. 'We must get you to safety.'

'Ah ... err ...' Tim didn't know how to tell his friend the bad news. 'Um, I think you should see this.'

'See what? I have no time to appreciate sculpture, no matter how fine it may be.'

'It's not that. It's ... Oh, please just come and look! It's urgent.'

Shrugging, Hercules stomped back to Tim. 'If you insist. What is this urgent thing I must see?'

Tim pointed mutely at the statues.

Humouring him, the hero stooped down and peered into their faces. A horrified groan left his lips and he sank to his knees.

'Noooo! I don't believe it. Agatha! Zoe!'
Hercules pawed at the figures in anguish.
'Why did I let you go unguarded? I am to
blame.'

'No you're not,' Tim hastened to say. 'It's Hera's fault. She tricked us and kept us imprisoned. There was no way you could have stopped it.'

'You are right. That evil witch is to blame. I shall have vengeance!' Hercules pulled himself to his feet, chin jutting aggressively. Dirt clung to his knees and his hair stood up in wild tufts. 'I shall return to the fortress and defeat Hera once and for all. You had better go now.'

'No way,' Tim said. He clutched the hero's tunic. 'I'm staying, I–.'

'Say no more. It is kind of you, but you cannot help us now. Go to your mother, Tim Baker. Go back to your own home, your own time. Lead a good life. It is what my dear wife would have wanted.' Tears welled in Hercules' eyes as he gazed down at Tim.

'Listen, I can help,' Tim insisted.

'After I have defeated Hera,' Hercules continued obliviously, 'I shall hunt Hades down and demand the return of my wife and daughter. He has taken loved ones from me before – he shall not do it again!'

'No, listen. Let's try the Golden Fleece gloves before you do anything else,' Tim said firmly. He didn't like the sound of Hercules picking a fight with the god of the dead. 'Zoe and I have one each. Mine's at home and hers is probably at your place. My vase is also–'

'Enough talking.' Hercules tucked his stone wife under one arm and his daughter under the other. 'Lead on, my friend.'

As soon as they reached the hero's house, Tim grabbed the vase's handles and ordered it to take him home. He left Hercules to search through Zoe's belongings for her glove.

The vase took him to his bedroom. Mum was out and the house was quiet. Tim opened his socks drawer and sifted quickly through it. The Golden Fleece glove wasn't there! Where had he put it? He flung open his other drawers and rummaged around. There was no sign of the glove. Biting his lip, Tim tried to

142

remember what he'd been wearing the last time he had it. His jeans? He ran down the stairs into the kitchen, praying that he hadn't left the glove in his pocket when he'd put the jeans into the washing machine. Mum always said to empty the pockets out first, but sometimes he forgot.

Tim opened the door of the washing machine and dragged out the damp but clean washing. He found his jeans, dug his fingers into his pocket … and pulled out the misshapen, scrunched up, sodden glove. It was no longer a sparkling gold. Rather, it was a dull mustard yellow.

'YAH!'

Tim yelped. He spread the glove out on the floor and tugged it back into shape. 'Please still work,' he said, hands shaking. What if he'd ruined it? Zoe and Agatha could stay frozen forever. Hercules would descend to the Underworld, pick a fight with Hades, and maybe never return.

He tried not to think about it. Tim had to take the glove back to Ancient Greece and hope that the Golden Fleece had not lost its magic.

Just as he was about to dash back up the stairs to fetch the vase, he heard a pounding at the front door. Tim looked over his shoulder and saw the unmistakable outline of Leo through the frosted glass window.

Well, there was no time to worry about that now.

Ignoring the knocking, Tim ran up the stairs.

Hercules' front door was already open when Tim arrived back in Ancient Greece, so he let himself in. Hercules was standing in the courtyard, where he'd placed the figures of Agatha and Zoe. The hero had found Zoe's Golden Fleece glove. He was trying to pull it over her stiff fingers, but he wasn't having much success.

'Help me, Tim Baker,' Hercules said, holding out the shining glove. 'My super-strong fingers were not made for such delicate tasks.'

Tim took the glove and deftly tugged it onto Zoe's stone hand. It was tricky, but he'd had a lot of practice when they'd rescued the crying statues. The glove sparkled and shone, and Tim watched intently for any sign of change.

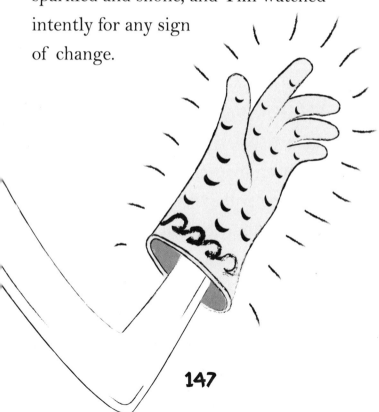

'IT'S NOT WORKING!'

Hercules howled.

'Give it time,' Tim said. It had taken a few minutes to revive the gorgon's statues too. He wasn't worried yet. He was more concerned about the other glove, which had been though the wash. Would it still work? He was about to find out.

'Put your glove on my wife,' Hercules said, jittering with impatience.

Tim pulled out the dull, damp glove. He said a silent prayer as he stretched it over Agatha's hand.

'Nothing is happening.' The hero stamped his foot.

'Check Zoe's wrist,' Tim said. He peered closely at her arm to see whether the stone was starting to turn the healthy colour of flesh.

It wasn't.

What had gone wrong? Surely Zoe's glove – the undamaged one – should work?

'The fleece is a fake,' Hercules roared. 'Who did you say sold it to you? Arachne? I shall crush that evil spider right now!' He picked up a ceramic pot and crunched it between his fingers, as if to demonstrate. 'I shall wrap her in her own web and hurl her off the highest mountain!' He threw the pot to the floor, where it shattered into tiny pieces. 'That'll teach her.'

'No. Wait. The fleece worked before; it should work again.' Tim dodged the flying pieces of crockery. He had a feeling he was doing something wrong.

He stared into Zoe's frozen face and thought he saw a glimmer of scorn in her stony gaze. 'What?' he whispered, wishing she could answer him. 'What am I doing wrong?'

His eyes swept over her, from head to foot. Everything was white and lifeless: her face, her body, her chiton, her long flowing ringlets. The only spot of colour was the golden glove.

Glove, singular.

They had used both gloves before – not just one! Maybe one alone wasn't enough to turn stone back into living flesh.

Hercules was busy finding more pots to crush, so Tim didn't waste time trying to explain. Instead, he tugged the damp glove off Agatha's hand and pulled it over Zoe's. 'C'mon, work,' he urged, as he stood back and watched. Surely a little detergent and water wouldn't destroy something as powerful and magical as the Golden Fleece?

It shouldn't.

It couldn't.

It hadn't!

The warm, living colour appeared first in Zoe's wrists, then began creeping

along her arms. It sped up as it moved
along. By the time it reached her
shoulders, the healthy glow started to
spread swiftly across her body. Before
long Zoe stood beside him in her bright

red chiton. She blinked and jerked, as if startled out of a deep sleep. Her eyes widened, awareness returning.

Without saying a word, Zoe tugged the gloves off her hands and pulled them onto her mother's. Hercules was still smashing pots and Tim had to jab him in the back to get his attention. Hercules spun around, arms raised, about to hurl a large oil jar across the courtyard. The jar fell with a crash at his feet. Overcome with emotion at the sight of his restored wife and child, the hero shouted with joy as he scooped them into the air.

'Hera did her worst, but we still managed to save you!' Tim crowed. 'She's losing her touch.'

Zoe squirmed until her father put her down. 'Hera? What did she have to do with it?'

Tim realised that Zoe didn't know about Hera's threat. 'She was going to set the last gorgon on me, but first she used it on you and your mum,' he explained.

'What gorgon? What are you talking about?'

'The one that turned you to stone, of course!'

'There was no gorgon,' Zoe said, taken aback. 'It was a man.'

Tim's eyebrows shot to the top of his head. 'Are you sure? What kind of man can turn people to stone?'

'Most likely it was a god,' Zoe said, 'but if so, it's one I've never seen before.'

Hercules, who had been listening, shook his head. 'You did not hear Hera's threat. It must have been the gorgon.'

'I'm perfectly aware of what I saw. Gorgons are female. He was a male. Either god or man.' Twisting around, Zoe looked to her mother for support. 'You saw him, didn't you, Ma?'

'No,' Agatha said shortly. She prodded Hercules' shoulder. 'You can put me down, too.'

Hercules did so, never moving his gaze away from Zoe. Father and daughter glared at each other with identical expressions of stubborn defiance, neither backing down.

'Do you think maybe the gorgon was just a bit manly?' Tim asked, groping for common ground.

'Don't be ridiculous,' Hercules and Zoe growled at him in unison. Then,

'YOU'RE ONE TO TALK!'

they shouted at each other.

'That's enough!' Agatha snapped. It wasn't like her to lose her temper, and the others looked at her in such surprise that she seemed to realise she was acting out of character. She paused, shook herself, and continued in a deliberately calmer voice.

'We need to work out a plan to make Hera leave us alone. Otherwise …' Agatha left the word hanging in the air, but Tim knew what she meant. Unless stopped, Hera would keep trying to hurt his friends and capture Tim, even if he was in his own time. None of them would ever be safe.

'I know!' Zoe chirped. 'We could tell her that Tim died in the battle!'

Tim was taken aback. 'That's a bit morbid, isn't it?'

'We must not tempt the Fates,' Agatha said. 'Maybe we should tell Hera the truth.'

Tim felt his heart sink as he realised what Agatha meant. 'That my mother's selling the vase and I can't come back, even if I want to? So … I'm no longer a threat?'

Agatha nodded and Zoe pressed her lips together, her eyes losing their shine.

Tim swallowed. 'I'd better go. You keep both gloves. Just in case Hera tries anything else after I'm gone.'

A loud honking sound made him jump. It was Hercules, blowing his nose on a huge handkerchief.

'I cannot take such sadness anymore,' the hero said. 'This is more emotion than I can handle in one day. I shall return to the battle and fight alongside Odysseus and Jason. Thumping a few hundred hoplites will make me feel better.' He got unsteadily to his feet. 'I

cannot say goodbye to you, Tim Baker.
Instead I will …'

Tim stared, stunned, as the great hero
Hercules stood to attention and saluted him.

Tim felt a surge of emotion when
Hercules saluted him. The hero
usually showed his affection with rib-
crushing hugs that lifted Tim right
off the ground. This was the first time
that Hercules had done something
like this. He was treating Tim like a
warrior – a hero. And here Tim was
feeling sorry for himself because had
to go home.

Tim sprang to his feet. 'I-I'll come with you,' he said thickly. 'Back to the fortress. I'll help you win the battle.'

'Oh no you will not,' Hercules said, dropping his arm back down. 'You will return home, where you will be safe.'

'What if I don't want to be safe?' Tim folded his arms and frowned at Hercules.

'What if I want you to be?' Hercules frowned back.

Zoe opened her mouth to say something when they heard voices at the door.

'I tell you, he will not be here.' The voice belonged to Odysseus. 'I'll warrant that he is seeking vengeance at this very moment, not hiding behind the skirts of his wife.'

'No, bro, he must have come here first.'
That had to be Jason.

They were back from the battle! It was over. Tim felt a surge of relief chase away his annoyance at Hercules. Now he wouldn't have to worry about abandoning his friends after all.

Still scowling at Tim, Hercules gestured for Zoe to let the guests in.

'Told you, bro,' Jason said as he strolled into the courtyard, a grin on his face.

Odysseus adjusted his boar tooth helmet and cleared his throat. 'We fought valiantly and defeated the goddess' mighty hoplites. Their job done well, we dismissed the dragon tooth soldiers, but I believe they are still standing outside awaiting instructions.'

The warrior looked at Hercules and raised a disapproving eyebrow. 'In the heat of the battle I looked for my brave friend, slayer of the fearsome Hydra. To my surprise, I found that he was nowhere in sight.'

'I had to remove Tim Baker from the battle before he could be turned to stone, and I had to check that my family were safe.'

'I thought you would be hunting down Hera, seeking your revenge. Instead you are here in the company of women and children.'

Hercules' face twisted. Given his reluctance to leave the battle, Tim knew how much that remark had hurt him. But the shame swiftly turned to anger.

Hercules bunched up his fists. 'Come over here and say that!'

'I shall!' Odysseus stormed over and halted inches from Hercules's face.

'Come on then!' Hercules said, shuffling his feet like a boxer in a ring.

'Ready when you are,' Odysseus said.

'I am ready now.'

'So am I.'

The two men began circling each other, shaking their fists, but neither seemed willing to throw the first punch.

Jason leant forward, his usual cool manner replaced by an ugly eagerness. 'Bros!' he urged, 'what are you waiting for?'

'Go on then,' Hercules taunted Odysseus. 'After you, coward.'

'All right then.'

'Fine.'

'Look, I am warning you …'

'No. I am warning you.'

'Oh, for goodness sake!' Tim thrust himself between the hero and the warrior, who both towered over him. 'This is ridiculous.' He felt like a teacher breaking up a fight in the school playground. 'I am the one who made Hercules leave,' he told Odysseus sternly. 'He didn't want to go.'

Hercules shot a triumphant glance at the warrior. Odysseus shifted his gaze to the ground and looked sullen.

'It's lucky that I did,' Tim continued, 'because Zoe and Agatha had been turned

166

to stone. Hercules and I rescued them.
He was just about to go back to help you
fight when you came charging in here. He
didn't run away. Understand?'

Odysseus grunted and shrugged.

'And the battle is over anyway, so
there's nothing to fight about is there?

IS THERE?'

he repeated more loudly, partly because
there'd been no reply, and partly because
he was getting angry again.

'No,' admitted Hercules.

'I suppose,' Odysseus agreed.

'So you can shake hands and make up,'
Tim said, stepping neatly out of the way.

Neither hero moved.

'I'm not going home until you make up,' Tim warned.

'Oh, all right.'

'Fine.'

Hercules and Odysseus grasped each other's wrists in a warrior's handshake and stared grimly into each other's faces. After a moment they cracked a smile, then started to pump their arms up and down, laughing and slapping each other on the back.

'That's better.' Tim wiped the sweat off his brow. Calming two angry Ancient Greeks was just as hard as stopping the Hydra's lopped off heads from growing back.

Their dispute forgotten, Hercules,

Odysseus and Jason retired to the andron, where they could discuss the battle in more detail. Tim watched them, a puzzled frown creasing his forehead. 'I know Hercules has a hot temper, but it's not usually that bad. It's almost like – I don't know. Like something's got into him. Odysseus, too.'

'Something has got into us all, I think,' agreed Agatha, who had been looking a little ashamed since her outburst.

'But what sort of something?' Tim asked.

Zoe looked thoughtful. Agatha shook her head. Neither had the answer.

Not wanting to draw his goodbyes out any longer than he had to, Tim gave

Agatha and Zoe one last hug. Without another word, he gripped the vase's handles and ordered it to take him home.

The vase deposited Tim in his bedroom.
He gazed at it sadly, trying to memorise
every detail of its glossy black body:
the picture of Hercules wrestling a
bull, the jagged ancient writing on the
back … A lump rose in his throat. Tim
knew he couldn't keep the vase with him
any longer. He had to put it back on the
mantelpiece in the living room, ready for
the buyer. Tim carried the vase solemnly

down the stairs, feeling as if he were part of a funeral procession.

This was it.

The end.

Soon he'd have nothing left of his adventures except for his memories.

'Hey, I can see you. Let me in!' Leo's voice startled Tim, nearly making him drop the vase. He tightened his grip. Mum would be devastated if he broke the vase a second time. She was counting on the money.

Leo had been hammering at the front door when he'd come back to get the Golden Fleece glove. Gritting his teeth, Tim went into the living room and placed the vase carefully on the mantelpiece. He gave it a final polish with his shirt sleeve before stepping back into the hallway.

Leo knocked again. 'Come on, Cinderella! Whaddya doing? Cleaning?' He pressed his nose against the frosted glass window, making it look even more like a pig's snout than usual.

Tim took a deep breath and let it out slowly. Leo didn't matter anymore, he realised. What was the worst thing he could do? Stop Tim from visiting the past? He couldn't go back anyway. All Leo could do was tease him, and Tim was used to that.

He squared his shoulders. 'Go away,' he called through the door. 'I'm busy.'

'We had a deal, remember?' Leo said. 'I beat you in chess fair and square. Now you gotta do something for me.'

'You never said what, though.' All Leo had said was that he was coming over. That didn't sound like much of a deal to Tim.

'Yeah, well I'm here to tell you now.' The pounding resumed. 'Let me in.'

'I don't think so.'

'Let me in or I'll smash your door down.'

Tim couldn't help grinning. 'Does that mean you'll huff and you'll puff–'

That was met with a volley of punches so fierce, Tim saw the door rattle in its frame. Curtains twitched in the houses across the road. Leo's racket was disturbing the neighbours.

Sighing, Tim opened the door. He wondered whether Leo had bruised his fist with all that knocking. Serve him right if he had.

'All right, come in. But you can't stay long. I'm busy.'

Leo didn't wait to be asked twice. He burst into the hallway. 'What-have-you-been-doing-with-that-vase?' he asked all in one breath.

'What vase?' Tim decided to stall for time while he worked out what to say.

'You know what vase! That old black thing. The one you told me had a snake in it, and it didn't. It's Ancient Egyptian or something.' Leo crinkled his nose.

'Oh that. It's Greek. Yeah, I've been

dusting it, that's all.'

Leo snorted. 'You were holding it that day when you vanished. I was here. I saw you. You were holding the vase, you disappeared, and then a couple of minutes later you were back.'

'What?' Tim shook his head in bewilderment, a puzzled smile plastered across his face. 'I've no idea what you're talking about.'

'When I came over to make the raft.' Leo was referring to the school project they'd had to do together. The model raft kept sinking, until Tim had the bright idea of asking Jason to fix it for them.

'You never told me how you made it look so good,' Leo continued. 'First it was a pile of twigs, then suddenly you had something that looked like it came from a shop.' His eyes widened. 'Did you steal it?'

'No, of course not.'

Leo stepped further into the house. 'Then how'd ya get it? Tell me, or I'll tell Miss Omiros you nicked it.'

Tim shuffled his feet. How would he get out of this one?

'I … um … had some help,' he answered truthfully.

'From who? Where? When? How'd ya get it done so quickly?' Leo fired questions so fast, Tim couldn't answer them even if he wanted to. Which he most certainly did not. 'It had something to do with that vase,' Leo went on. 'I know it. I'm not as dumb as you think I am.'

Tim folded his arms and shook his head. Leo couldn't force him to answer.

'When I was here,' Leo said, 'I heard you say something. First I thought you were talking to yourself, which didn't surprise me cos you're a nutcase. But I've been thinking. You were talking to that vase. You were telling it what to do.'

Tim forced himself not to show any reaction. 'You were dreaming,' he said, shrugging as if he couldn't care less what Leo thought.

'Dreaming, was I? I'll show you dreaming. Where'd you put it?' Leo pushed Tim roughly out of the way, then went barrelling down the hallway. He stomped into the living room, flinging open cupboard doors as he went. 'Hah! Found it.'

Tim followed hot on his heels.

Leo's legs were longer than his, and he reached the mantelpiece before Tim could catch him. Leo paused for a moment, as if preparing himself, then he grabbed the vase's handles.

'Oi, vase,' Leo grunted. 'Take me where you take Tim.'

A golden mist shimmered around Leo's feet. It swirled higher, growing thicker and brighter. This couldn't be happening! Yelping, Tim hurled himself at Leo. He caught hold of the vase just as it started to lift Leo off the ground.

Tim gasped as they both rose up into the air. It looked like he was going back to Ancient Greece after all, and this time he had company!

Look out for Tim's next ADVENTURE!

HOPELESS HEROES

HADES' PET
HELLHOUND

STELLA
TARAKSON

Sweet
Cherry

Tim Baker couldn't believe what was happening. He was flying – hurtling through time and space – with Leo the bully, of all people.

Leo had figured out Tim's secret. Not all of it, but enough to make him determined to ferret out the rest. First he'd overheard Tim talking to the old Greek vase. Then, while Leo watched, a golden mist had appeared, completely covering Tim and the vase. When the mist lifted, both had vanished.

Tim had hoped that Leo would forget what he'd seen, or at least think that he'd imagined it. No such luck. Like a pit bull with a trouser leg, Leo hadn't let go. Realising that Tim had been ordering the vase to take him somewhere, Leo had finally blustered his way into Tim's home, grabbed the vase, and ordered it to take him wherever it took Tim. Now they were both headed for Ancient Greece.

The wind roared in Tim's ears as they flew through the air. He stole a glance at Leo's face. The boy's eyes were wide as he tried to see through the golden mist surrounding them. Tim had to admire his

courage. The first time he'd travelled with the vase, Tim had been so scared that he kept his eyes clamped shut.

'What's happening?' Leo shouted.

'You'll see.'

Tim's adventures had begun when he accidentally broke the old Greek vase, and Hercules had emerged from the pieces. The hero had been trapped for thousands of years by the wicked goddess Hera, and quickly became firm friends with Tim. It was Hercules' encouragement that had finally helped Tim to stand up to Leo – something Tim would always be grateful for.

Gone were the days when Tim felt awkward and uncertain. In Ancient Greece especially, he was a better, stronger person. Nobody called him Cinderella, the nickname Leo had invented to tease him about housework. People in the past thought Tim was brave and clever. He'd been called a hero by the goddess Athena!

'See what? You'd better tell me, Cinderella.'

Tim pressed his lips together. As happy as he always was to see his Ancient Greek friends, how could he unleash Leo on them?

When Hercules had escaped the vase into the modern world, he'd been invisible to everyone except Tim. The hero had even knocked Leo down once, much to the angry boy's confusion. But Hercules wasn't invisible anymore. Leo would put two and two together and get five: five fingers, in a fist, straight into Tim's face. Then Hercules would seek revenge, Zoe would get involved, and all hell would break loose. Tim shuddered.

Leo didn't know it, but the vase had to obey his every command. The spell "He who holds me commands me" was written on it in Ancient Greek. By grabbing the vase, Leo had put himself in control – and Tim was powerless to stop him.

Or was he? He was holding the vase, too …

Maybe he could reverse Leo's order.

'Oh vase,' Tim said, ignoring Leo's glare, 'take us back home.'

Never before had Tim changed instructions mid-flight. The vase paused. It wobbled, as if uncertain what to do.

'Hey, no!' Leo shouted. 'Take us where Tim goes.' The vase started moving forwards again.

'I said take us home!' The vase started to reverse.

'FORWARDS!'

shouted Leo, at the exact same moment
that Tim shouted

'BACKWARDS!'

The vase went neither backwards
nor forwards. It shuddered to a halt. It
hovered in the air for a moment. Then it
plunged straight down.

Tim clung desperately to the vase as it plummeted. This had never happened before! They must have confused it by giving conflicting instructions. Like an angry horse, the vase was trying to shake them off.

'Dude!' Leo shouted. 'What have you done?'

'It's not my fault!' Tim cried.

'Is too! I'm gonna get you for this.'

If the ground didn't get them first, Tim thought grimly. What was the point of arguing? Right now it didn't matter whose fault it was.

'Oh vase,' Tim ordered, forcing himself to stay calm. 'Take us home.'

'No way! Oi vase, take us where you take Tim.'

The vase dropped even faster.

'Are you mad?' Tim squeaked. 'We're confusing it. We have to tell it the same thing.'

'You just don't want me to know where you go!' Leo shouted over the sound of the rushing wind.

'VASE, TAKE US

HOME. NOW!'

A look of anger crossed Leo's face and Tim felt a stab of fear. What if the other boy tried to push him off? Then Leo could make the vase take him to Ancient Greece alone. He'd meet Zoe and Hercules and Agatha. He might pick a fight with them. Or worse, he might become friends with them! He might take Tim's place, and his friends would forget all about him.

Tim shuddered. Best not to think about it. He held on to the slippery handle as if his life depended on it. Which it did. Maybe, for safety's sake, he should let Leo have his way. The vase would land at Zoe's house. Then, once Tim had a chance to think, he could work out what to do.

'You win,' Tim said. 'Vase, take us to Zoe's house.'

But the vase continued to fall.

'I said take us to Zoe's!' Tim squeaked in panic.

'PLEASE!'

It didn't work. They had lost control. As if sulking, the vase accelerated. Tim closed his eyes. Hopefully it would slow down and give them a soft landing, at least. Goodness knows where – and when – they'd end up.

'Hey, little buddy. What are you doing up here?'

Tim's eyes snapped open. The messenger god Hermes hovered beside

him, the wings on his cap flapping vigorously. The god's lips curled into a crooked grin as he matched his descent to the vase's.

'Help!' Tim cried. 'The vase has gone mad!'

'Who's your friend?' Hermes nodded

at Leo, whose eyes bulged at the sight of the flying god.

'I'll explain later,' Tim said. 'Hurry!'

Hermes swiftly snatched one of Tim's hands with his right hand, and one of Leo's with his left. They immediately stopped falling. 'Keep hold of the vase,' Hermes warned. 'Don't want to break it again, do we?'

Tim felt weak with relief. He never knew what to make of Hermes. Although the young god served Hera, sometimes he seemed to be on Tim's side. And now he'd saved his life! It was very confusing.

With a nod and a wink, Hermes deposited them on Zoe's doorstep. 'Catch ya later,' he said, before flapping away.

Tim couldn't help noticing that the god's flight wasn't as smooth as usual. It was lopsided, like a sprinter running with a sprained ankle. Had he sprained one of his wings?

Tim shook himself. He didn't have time to worry about Hermes' wings now. He had bigger problems.

Tim tugged at the vase and Leo surrendered it without a struggle. He was too busy gaping at the row of simple mud-brick buildings, which were so unlike anything at home.

'Where did you bring us, Cinderella? It isn't even London!'

'We're not in Kansas anymore, Toto,' Tim replied, quoting from *The Wizard of Oz*.

'Then where on earth are we? Hey!
I bet this isn't even Earth!' Leo took a
menacing step towards Tim. 'This is
another planet, isn't it? That flying guy's
an alien.'

'We're not–'

'Gimme that vase. I'm going home
before they start experimenting on me.'

Tim tucked the vase behind his back.
'Of course this is Earth,
dummy.'

'Oh yeah? Then explain
the flying guy.'

Tim clenched his
fists. 'I'm not explaining
anything. I didn't ask you
to come. Why couldn't you

just mind your own business?'

'Who lives here?' Leo pointed at Zoe's house. 'Can they fly, too?'

'My friends. And no, they can't fly.'

'Friends? Since when do you have friends?' Leo snorted. 'Other than that prat Ajay.'

Tim didn't bother answering. He had no intention of sharing his Greek friends with someone who'd forced their way into his secret world.

'Look, this is what we're going to do.' Tim made his voice sound strong. 'We're going to take a handle each, and *I* will order the vase to take us home. You're going to forget all about this. If you don't, I'll set that flying guy on you.'

Leo snorted. 'Nice try, Cinderella. If *you* don't want me here, then I'm staying. You're just scared that your friends will like me more than they like you.'

'Don't be ridiculous,' Tim said, even though that was exactly what he was thinking. 'What happens if I knock on that door right now?' Leo lifted his beefy fist to bang on Zoe's front door.

'Oh no you don't!' Tim threw himself at Leo and gripped his fist with both hands.

Grunting and cursing, the boys wrestled on the doorstep: Tim trying to pull Leo away from the house, while Leo kept hurling himself back towards it.

'Quiet,' Tim hissed. 'They'll hear us!'

'Well in that case …' Leo took a deep breath and shouted,

'OI! OPEN UP!'

'Shut up!'

'Make me.'

Tim tried. Reaching over, he clamped his hand over the boy's mouth. But it was too late. Tim and Leo froze mid-tussle as the front door opened.

HOPELESS HEROES

To download Hopeless Heroes

ACTIVITIES
AND
POSTERS

visit:
www.sweetcherrypublishing.com/resources

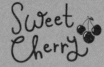